This ColoringBook
Belongs To:

_ _ _ _ _ _ _ _ _ _ _ _ _

ANGRY BULL

AZTEC CAMELION

CroCO SMITH

LIGHT FEATHER CROW

LANCER FOX

NUBO_FROG

SAMURAI_FROG

High Knight GOAT

RAMBO GORILLA

KITTY

EL MATADOR LAMA

MONKEY KING

ORCA The GREY

FIERCE OWL

BEAROVITCH

ITTO_RYU_RABBIT

AKA_PANDA

RHINO_Knight

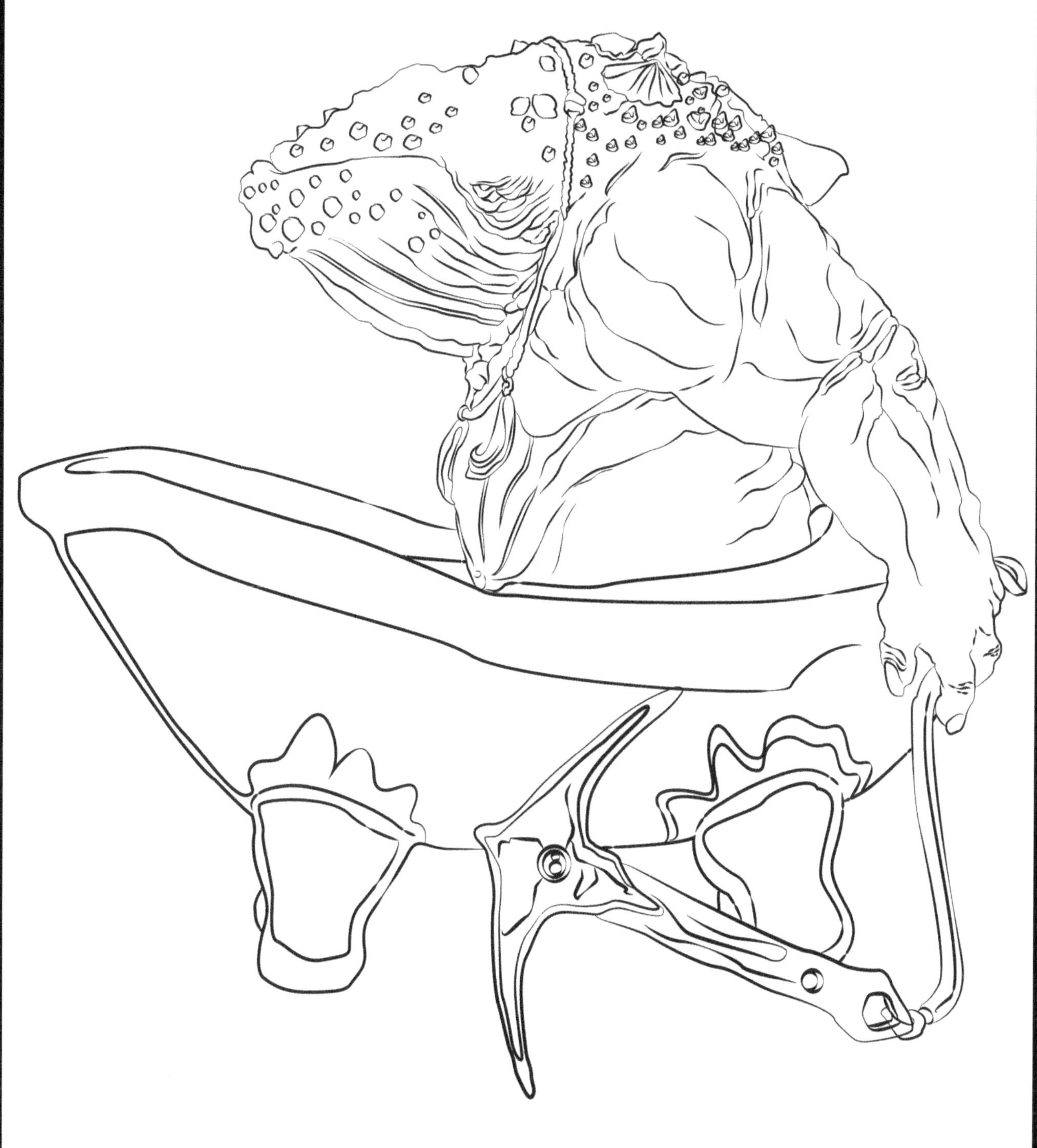

WALE BLAZE

WOLFEY